Star Boy's Surprise

Written by Jana Hunter

Illustrated by Mark Turner

Far, far away, in deep, dark space, was a star.
From far away, that star was just a tiny twinkle.

But close up, it was sand and sea and sparkling red rocks.
And on it lived Star Boy and his robot, Ace.
That was it.
Just one boy, one robot and lots of pink sand.

My mate!

Mate, mate.

Star Boy and Ace did everything together.
If Star Boy raced across the sparkly sand,
Ace raced with him.
If Star Boy chased a falling star,
Ace chased with him.

If Star Boy shut his eyes,
Ace shut down too.
Ace was just a robot but
Star Boy knew he was the best robot ever!

5

The trouble was, Ace was a robot.
He couldn't think up a game,
have an idea, or even surprise Star Boy.
Ace couldn't help it.
It was just the way he was made.

It was the day before Star Boy's birthday.
Alone on his star, there was just one thing Star
Boy wanted ...

... A SURPRISE!

A big, birthday surprise.

How could a robot surprise a boy?

How could rocks or sand or sea surprise him?

There was not much hope ...

... but Star Boy had hope –

a tiny twinkle of hope deep inside him.

After all, around him there were stars,
and Star Boy knew about stars.
So, closing his eyes,
Star Boy wished upon a star.

Then Star Boy went to
sleep and Ace shut down
with him.
A boy and his robot,
alone on a star,
dreaming a birthday
dream.

When Star Boy woke up on his birthday,
the sun was shining.
He was about to sing "Happy Birthday"
to himself when Star Boy saw
that Ace had gone.
Ace gone! That wasn't the surprise
he was hoping for!

Star Boy looked everywhere but
Ace was nowhere to be found.
Star Boy climbed a big rock.
"Oh, why did I wish for a surprise?"
he cried out. "I had Ace!"
Then Star Boy saw tracks in the wet sand
behind the rock.
From far away he heard the
click, click, click of robot wheels …

… *"ACE!"*

There was Ace, rolling up and down the beach.

What was he up to?

Star Boy watched as Ace collected rocks.

Click, click went his robot arms as

he picked up blue rocks, green rocks,

purple, pink and gold.

What a surprise!

Star Boy watched as Ace laid the
rocks down in long, neat rows.
Row after sparkling row,
twinkling in the sunlight.
What was he doing?

Surprise, surprise.

13

Ace was making huge letters
with the rows of rocks.
Letters that from far away spelt out …

And from far, far away
Space Girl read
Ace's birthday wishes.

"Hey!" Space Girl said to her robot, Zar.
"It's someone's birthday!"
"Birthday, birthday," bleeped Zar.
"LET'S PARTY!" said Space Girl
and she zoom-zoomed around …

… to land right on Star Boy's twinkling star!
"Wow!" gasped Star Boy.
"Happy birthday!" laughed Space Girl,
jumping down from her rocket.
"I read your sign."

16

Ace, you're the best!

Best, best.

Star Boy looked at the huge letters and suddenly he understood Ace's birthday surprise.

Together Star Boy and Space Girl,
Ace and Zar had the best birthday party ever ...

... rocking and rolling on the sand,
singing out to the stars and
flashing their lights.
They ate Moon Munchies and Comet Chips,
then Space Ices and Jupiter Juice.

Just when Star Boy thought it was all over,
Ace and Zar rolled up with a birthday cake –
a huge cake sprinkled with moon dust icing.
Space Girl took some pictures with her space
viewer.
They sang "Happy Birthday" to Star Boy.
"This birthday has been one surprise
after another!" he laughed.

"Come back to my planet," said Space Girl.
"It's full of surprises."
"Just like Ace!" Star Boy hugged Ace.
Ace blinked. "More, more," he bleeped and
everyone laughed.

The four friends zoomed off into space,
with Ace's birthday surprise
sparkling below them.

Pictures from Space Girl's Viewer

From Space Girl's Rocket

At the Party

🐾 Ideas for guided reading 🐾

Learning objectives: Taking account of punctuation in reading aloud with appropriate expression; using awareness of grammar to decipher new or unfamiliar words; understanding speech marks in reading; speaking with clarity and intonation when reading and reciting texts

Curriculum links: Citizenship: Taking part – developing skills of communication and participation

Interest words: surprise, dream, gasped, laughed

Word count: 645

Getting started

This book can be read over two sessions

- Ask the children to look at the cover illustration and read the title. Ask pairs to discuss what they think the 'surprise' is.
- Ask children to turn to pp4–5 and comment on the relationship between Star Boy and Ace. Turn to pp6–7. Skim read the text to see what Star Boy's problem is. Ask pairs to discuss how they would feel celebrating a birthday with only a robot for company.
- Return to earlier predictions about the 'surprise' – do the children still believe they are right?
- Return to the beginning, explaining that you are going to read the first two pages aloud to model the correct phrasing and expression. Can the children say how you knew where to pause?

Reading and responding

- Ask children to read the story silently, at their own pace. Ask them to think about how punctuation helps them to read and understand the story.
- 'Listen-in' to individuals reading aloud in turn and observe their ability to tackle unfamiliar words.